one woolly wombat

Written by Rod Trinca and Kerry Argent

Illustrated by Kerry Argent

A CRANKY NELL BOOK

Kane/Miller
BOOK PUBLISHERS

First American Paperback Edition, 1987

First American Edition 1985 by Kane/Miller Book Publishers
La Jolla, California

Originally published in Australia by Omnibus Books in 1982

For information, contact
Kane/Miller Book Publishers
P.O. Box 8515
La Jolla, CA 92038

Library of Congress Cataloging Publication Data

Trinca, Rod. One woolly wombat.

"A Cranky Nell book"
Summary: Humorous illustrations depict fourteen
Australian animals, introduced in rhyme, along with
the numbers from one to fourteen.
1. Children's stories, Australian. [1. Zoology — Australia — Fiction.
2. Australia — Fiction. 3. Counting. 4. Stories in rhyme]
I. Argent, Kerry, 1960– ill. II. Title.
PX8.3.T6950n 1985 [E] 84-21854
ISBN-13: 978-0-916291-10-5
ISBN-10: 0-916291-10-3

Printed and Bound in China by Regent Publishing Services Ltd.

11 12 13 14 15 16 17 18 19 20

one woolly wombat

one woolly wombat sunning by the sea

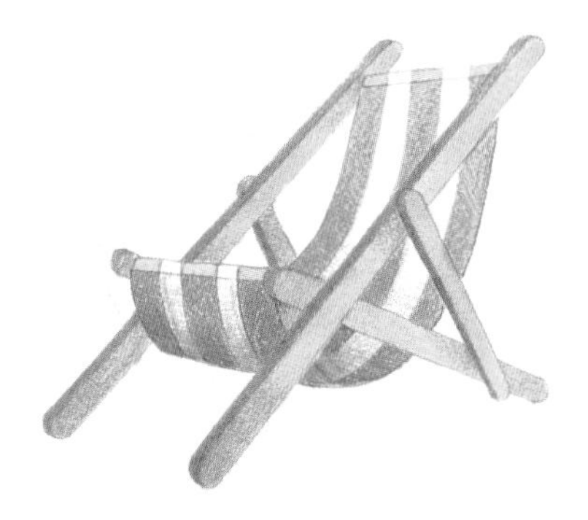

two cuddly koalas sipping gumnut tea

three warbling magpies waking up the sun

four thumping kangaroos dancing just for fun

five pesky platypuses splashing with their feet

six cheeky possums looking for a treat

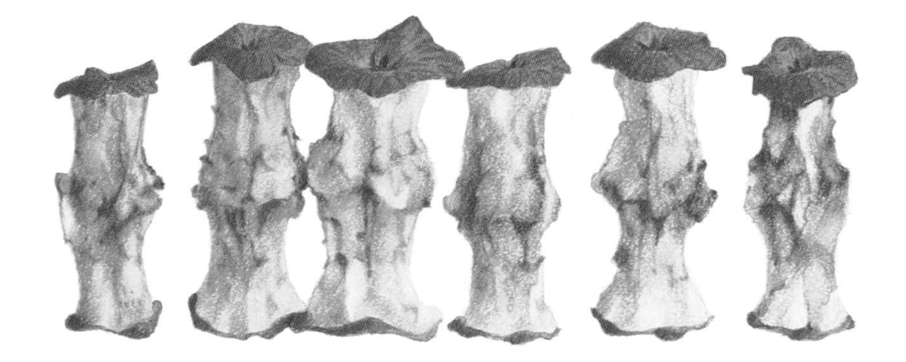

seven emus running . . . in and out the bush

FOOTBALL

eight spiky echidnas eating ants — whoosh

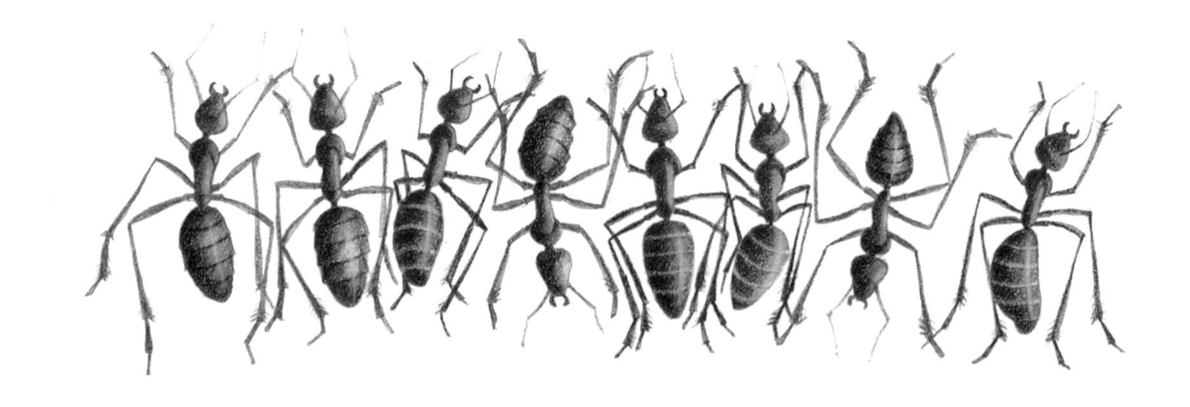

nine hungry goannas wondering what to cook

Gecko Stew
Cookery for Goannas
GOANNA RECIPES
COOKERY – The Goanna

ten giggly kookaburras writing riddle books

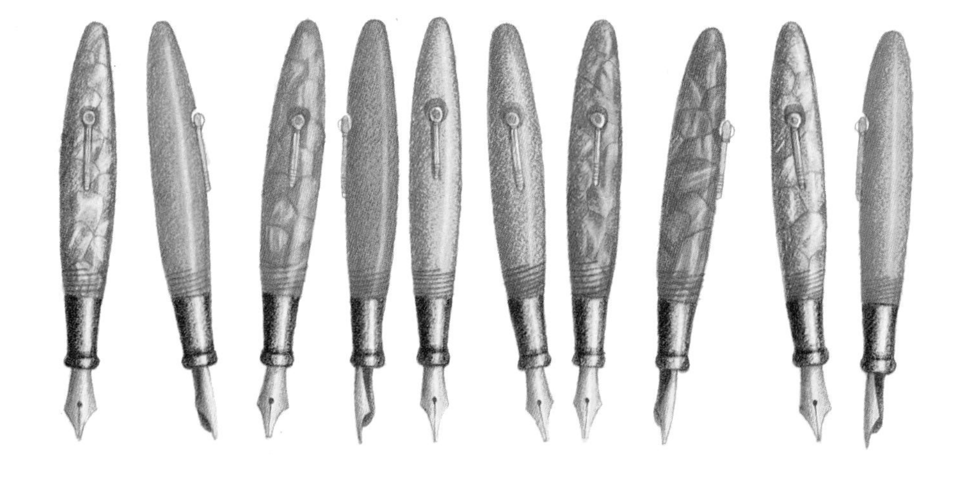

SPECIAL
DRYING

eleven dizzy dingoes twirling with their paws

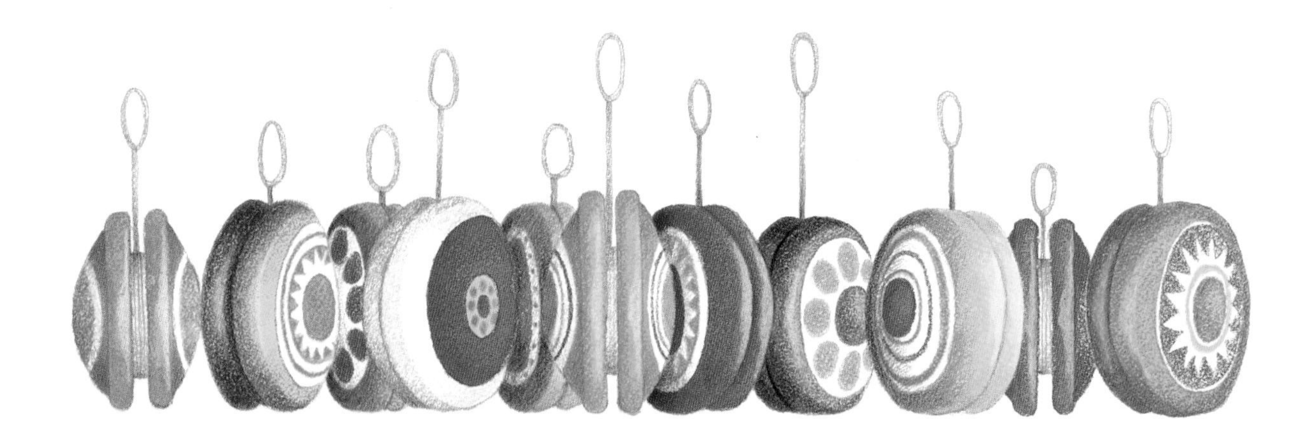

twelve crazy cockatoos counting on their claws

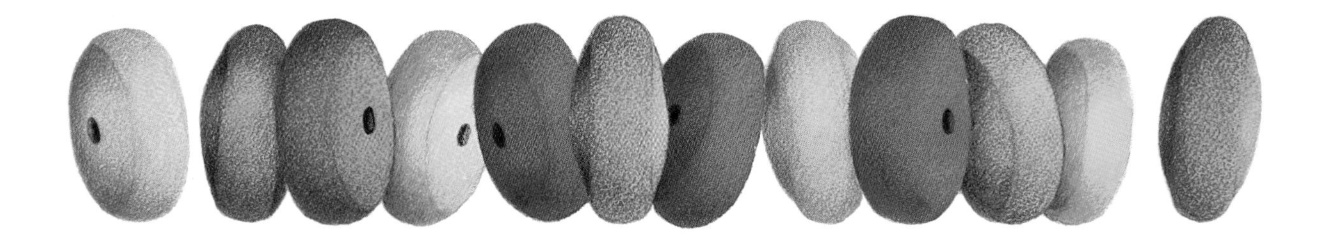

thirteen hopping mice picking desert pea

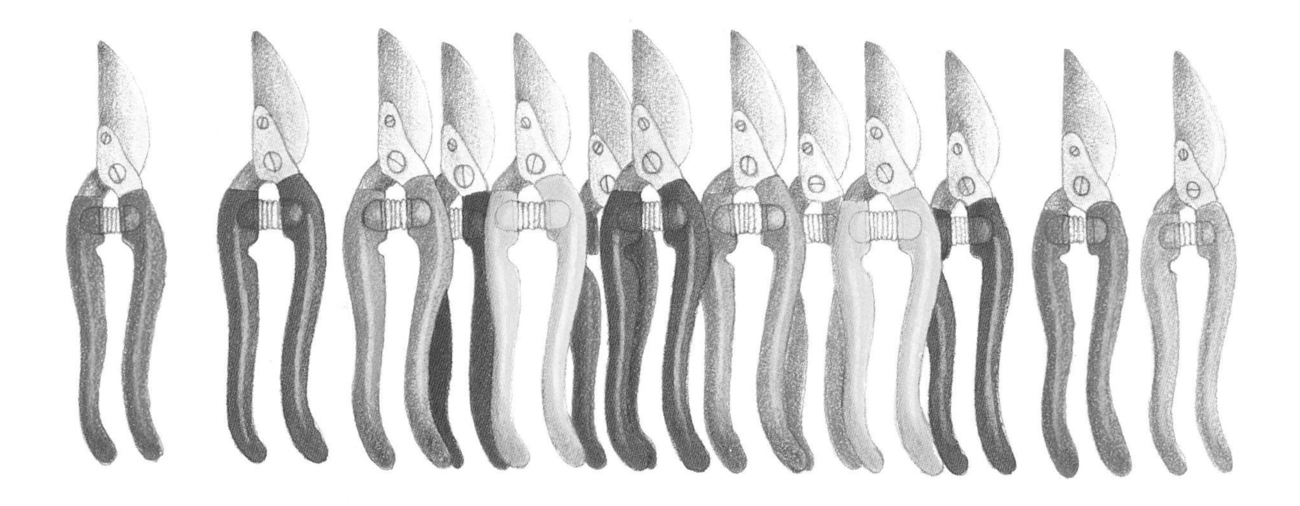

fourteen slick seals sailing out to sea

SOUTHERN CROSS
SEAL